Jeremy Strong

Giant Jim and the Hurricane

Illustrated by Nick Sharratt

PUFFIN BOOKS

PUFFIN BOOKS

Published by the Penguin Group
Penguin Books Ltd, 80 Strand, London WC2R 0RL, England
Penguin Putnam Inc., 375 Hudson Street, New York, New York 10014, USA
Penguin Books Australia Ltd, 250 Camberwell Road, Camberwell, Victoria 3124, Australia
Penguin Books Canada Ltd, 10 Alcorn Avenue, Toronto, Ontario, Canada M4V 3B2
Penguin Books India (P) Ltd, 11 Community Centre, Panchsheel Park, New Delhi – 110 017, India
Penguin Books (NZ) Ltd, Cnr Rosedale and Airborne Roads, Albany, Auckland, New Zealand
Penguin Books (South Africa) (Pty) Ltd, 24 Sturdee Avenue, Rosebank 2196, South Africa

Penguin Books Ltd, Registered Offices: 80 Strand, London WC2R 0RL, England

www.penguin.com

First published by Viking 1997
Published in Puffin Books 1999
16

Text copyright © Jeremy Strong, 1997
Illustrations copyright © Nick Sharratt, 1997
All rights reserved

The moral right of the author and illustrator has been asserted

Set in Baskerville

Made and printed in England by Clays Ltd, St Ives plc

British Library Cataloguing in Publication Data
A CIP catalogue record for this book is available from the British Library

ISBN 0-140-38248-8

www.greenpenguin.co.uk

For Poppy

Contents

1 How to Arrest a Giant 1

2 Homeless and Hopeless 22

3 A Bed for the Night 37

4 Disasters Everywhere 51

5 Help! 66

1 How to Arrest a Giant

There was a very strange noise coming from beyond the window. Constable Dunstable sat up in bed and scratched his head. It was half-past six in the morning. What could be making such a noise? He got out of bed, went across to the window and pulled back the curtains.

'Aargh!' Constable Dunstable leaped
back. Staring through the window at him
was a huge face, with a ginger beard as
big as a forest and –

the face belonged to a head, and
the head belonged to a body, and
the body had two long, hairy arms,
and two huge legs.

'It's a giant!' cried Constable Dunstable. He ran downstairs and ran across the room. He opened his front door and ran outside, right between the giant's legs, and he carried on running and running, still in his pyjamas.

'There's a giant in our town!' yelled Constable Dunstable as he hurried through the streets.

Windows were thrown open. Sleepy people poked out their heads to see what all the fuss was about.

'Well I never!' murmured Mrs Sniffling. 'Constable Dunstable is running round the streets in his pyjamas. He is shouting something about a giant.'

'A giant?' sniffed Mr Sniffling, and he sat up in bed. 'I don't believe in giants.'

'I think you might believe in this one,' said his wife. 'Because this giant is

standing at the end of our road. He is as tall as four houses sitting on top of each other, and he is holding a giant saucepan in one hand and a giant wicker basket in the other, and he has a giant saxophone strapped to his back.'

Mr Sniffling growled and climbed out of his nice, warm bed. He went to the window. 'Oh!' he cried. 'A giant! There's a giant in our town!'

'Do you know, that is exactly what Constable Dunstable was saying,' said Mrs Sniffling. 'Look, now *you* are running round in your pyjamas too!'

It was quite true. Mr Sniffling was racing down the street in his pyjamas. In fact, almost half the town were rushing about in pyjamas and nightdresses, and they were all shouting at each other.

'A giant! A giant! We shall all be squashed!' cried Mr Sniffling.

'We shall all be squished!' squeaked Mrs Goodbody. She hurried across to

Constable Dunstable. 'Arrest that giant at once!' she insisted.

Constable Dunstable looked up at the giant's big, ginger head and swallowed hard. He was an awfully big person to arrest.

'I shall have to put my uniform on and get my handcuffs and my *Giant-Spotter's Handbook*. Then you can all come with

me and we will arrest the giant and shoo
him out of our town. We don't want
giants here.'

'No! We don't want giants in our
town!' everyone shouted.

'What's wrong with giants?' asked
little Poppy Palmer, the farmer's
daughter. But nobody listened. She
thought the giant looked rather nice.

The crowd marched off behind
Constable Dunstable and waited
patiently until the policeman had
changed into his uniform. When
Constable Dunstable came back out they
all got up and marched behind him once
again, and that helped him feel a bit
braver.

They went up the road and there was the giant, standing at the other end and frowning down at them with his great big, bearded face. The crowd stopped.

Mr Sniffling pushed Constable Dunstable forward.

'Go on,' he muttered. 'Arrest that giant at once.'

Constable Dunstable took two wobbly steps forward and then stopped. He pressed his knees together very hard, so that he couldn't hear them knocking any longer. He stared up and UP and UP.

'I arrest you in the name of the law!'
he cried. 'Put on these handcuffs at
once!'

The giant looked at the tiny handcuffs.
They were much too small for his great
hands. Carefully he put down his
saucepan and his wicker basket and
gently held out his hands. Constable
Dunstable just managed to push the
handcuffs over the tips of the giant's
fingers. He snapped them shut.

'There,' said Constable Dunstable.
'Now you are our prisoner. I am going to
put you in jail for years and years and
years.'

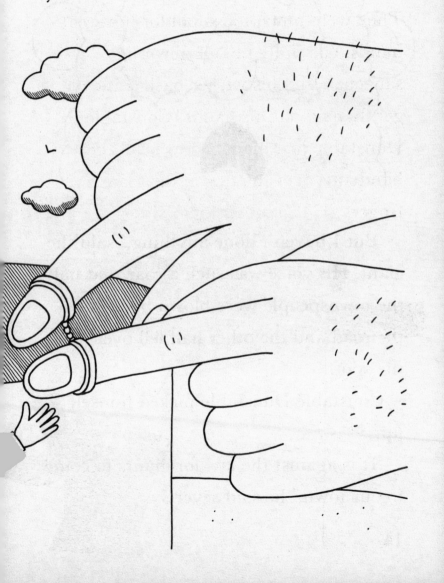

'But I haven't done anything,' said the giant. His voice was such a roar that half the townspeople were blown back down the road and the other half fell over on the spot.

Constable Dunstable picked himself up.

'It is against the law for giants to come to our town,' he said severely.

14

'That isn't very fair,' said the giant,
and everyone fell over again. Constable
Dunstable picked himself up.

'AND – you keep knocking everyone
over.'

'I can't help it,' said the giant, and
everyone fell over again. Constable
Dunstable picked himself up for the third
time.

'Then I shall have to put you in jail
for ever and ever!' said the policeman.

And that was when the giant began to cry. Huge tears filled his eyes, trickled down his cheeks and crashed to the ground far below.

'Stop it!' cried the soaking townspeople. 'We shall all drown!'

This made the giant cry even more, and it was just like two long, thin, sparkling waterfalls. The giant cried for half the morning. Soon there was a little pool of tears, and the pool became a pond, and the pond became a lake. Some people got out their umbrellas and some people got out their boats, but the children got out their swimming costumes and swam about splashing each other.

Mrs Careless, the Mayoress, was becoming most concerned. 'We can't have this,' she told Constable Dunstable.

'We must do something. This lake will start overflowing any minute and then the whole town will be flooded. Tell the giant you won't arrest him if he stops crying.'

So Constable Dunstable told the giant to stop crying.

'I won't arrest you,' he explained. 'But you must promise to be a good giant.'

'I am a good giant,' snivelled the giant, and he blew his nose –

SSPPPPLLLLLUUUURRRRRGGGGHHH!

– and everyone who wasn't swimming
fell over, and half the rowing boats were
overturned, and Constable Dunstable
disappeared into the lake.

'I have always been a good giant,' the giant added, poking a helpful finger into the lake and hooking Constable Dunstable back on to dry land.

'Do you think you could speak more softly?' asked Mrs Goodbody. 'Every time you speak it makes a terrible wind and we all fall over. And please don't sneeze.'

'Sorry,' said the giant, and everyone fell over.

'Sorry,' he said again, very quietly, and everyone picked themselves up.

The policeman glared angrily at the giant.

'Right then, you sit down on that hill. You are going to have to answer some questions.'

'Oh good! Is it a quiz, like on television? Will I win a painting set?'

asked the giant, sitting himself down on the hill with an enormous, thunderous thump.

'Not exactly. First of all, question one: What is your name?'

'Jim.'

'I want your full name,' said the policeman.

'Oh. Giant Jim.'

'Question two: Where do you live?'

'That's obvious,' said Giant Jim with such a big smile that his whole beard went crinkly. 'I live right here.'

2 Homeless and Hopeless

'Here!' cried everyone else. 'In our town?'

'Well, I would like to live here,' said Giant Jim. 'It's nice here. You've got a lake and everything.'

'We didn't have a lake until you came here and started crying,' sniffed Mr Sniffling.

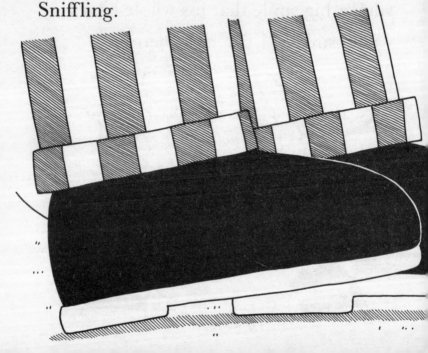

'But it *is* a nice lake,' said Poppy Palmer. 'We can go rowing and swimming and sail our boats.'

'You might fall in,' warned the children's mothers.

'We like falling in!' shouted the children.

'I am not at all sure about this,' said Constable Dunstable. 'Giants can be very dangerous. How do we know that you won't eat anyone?'

Giant Jim looked most hurt. 'Of course I won't eat anyone. I don't eat meat. I'm a vegetable.'

'I think you mean that you are a vegetarian,' said Poppy Palmer.

The giant grinned. 'That's right. I'm a vegenariable!'

'Well, I don't know,' grumbled Constable Dunstable, and he got out his *Giant-Spotter's Handbook*. He thumbed through the pages.

'Have you only got one eye? No? You're not a Cyclops then. Have you got a golden harp and a hen?'

'I don't have a golden harp, but I do have a hen!' cried the giant. 'You are clever! How did you know that? I have a hen in my wicker basket here,' and he tapped the big basket.

Constable Dunstable took several steps back.

'If you've got a hen then you could be a Beanstalk Giant. My book says that Beanstalk Giants are very, very dangerous. They eat humans.'

The giant looked heartbroken and he shook his head sadly. 'But I don't eat people. I eat vegetables and eggs. That's why I have my hen. Her name is Florence Fluffybum and she lays eggs for me. I put them in my saucepan and I have scrambled eggs, boiled eggs, or maybe an omelette or egg-bread . . .'

'Yes, yes, all right,' muttered the

policeman. 'You're not a Beanstalk Giant then. How about a Big Friendly Giant? Do you do dreams? Is that a dream-puffer strapped to your back?'

The giant shook his head.

'No, this is my saxophone.'

Constable Dunstable turned over the page and his face lit up.

'Ah! Now I've got you! If that's a saxophone then you must be a Jazz Giant!'

'A Jazz Giant,' murmured Giant Jim. 'I'm a Jazz Giant.'

'That's right. And my book says that Jazz Giants are harmless, cheerful, but often noisy, especially if they play the drums.'

'I don't play the drums. I play the saxophone,' said Jim with a big smile. He swung his saxophone across his front.

A moment later the air was shattered by an explosion of music and everybody fell over yet again.

The nearby trees had half their leaves blown off. The terrified sheep ran round their field so fast that the sheep at the front caught up with the sheep at the back and they all collided in a big heap. The cows tumbled on to their backs and waved their legs in the air, with their udders wobbling about like big, pink jellies.

'Stop! Stop!' yelled Constable Dunstable, with both hands clasped over his ears.

Giant Jim put down his saxophone.

'Did you like that?' he grinned. 'I'm a very good saxophone player.'

The townspeople struggled back to their feet, shaking their ringing heads. 'You *are* a very good saxophone player,' they agreed. 'But please don't play so loudly.'

'It was brilliant!' yelled the children, who always liked a free disco.

Constable Dunstable was rather relieved that Giant Jim did not play the drums. After all, if the giant saxophone knocked everybody off their feet, giant drums would probably start an earthquake. However, he still had some important questions to ask.

'Where are you going to live?' he wanted to know.

The giant gazed down at Poppy Palmer. 'I'd like to live with you,' he said.

'Oh!' said Poppy. 'That's nice, but our house is too small for you.'

'It's a farmhouse,' grunted Mr Palmer the farmer. 'It's for farmers.'

'Then I shall live with you!' said Giant Jim, pointing at Constable Dunstable.

'No, you can't,' said the policeman firmly. 'I live in the Police House and it's just for policemen.'

'In that case,' smiled Giant Jim, 'if the Farmhouse is for farmers, and the Police House is for policemen, I shall live in the Giant House.'

Everyone looked at each other.

'The Giant House?' they muttered.

Wherever was the Giant House? Constable Dunstable frowned.

'We haven't got a Giant House, because giants have never lived here. You are homeless and you will have to sleep outside on the hills until you find a house for yourself. Now, be very careful where you tread because you are big and everything else round here is small and you don't fit in.'

With that, Constable Dunstable set off back to the town and everyone followed, except for Poppy Palmer and her best friend, Crasher. (He was called Crasher because he ran around so fast that he kept crashing into things. He also crashed *out* of things – like trees, when he was halfway up them.)

Giant Jim stared after the disappearing townspeople.

'I'm homeless,' he muttered. 'Everybody has a home except me. I'm homeless and hopeless.'

'There's nothing wrong with you,' said Crasher, trying to cheer up the giant.

'Oh yes there is. My feet are too big . . .'

'They *are* quite large,' agreed the children.

'And my legs are too big . . .'

'They are a bit like tree trunks,' nodded Crasher.

'And my chest is too big . . .'

'It is – huge!' murmured Poppy.

'And my head is too big.'

Poppy and Crasher looked at each other. 'You are *very* big,' they said.

'But that doesn't mean that you are hopeless,' said Poppy. 'I bet you can do lots of things. You've already made us a lake.'

'I didn't mean to,' said Giant Jim.

'I know, but it's a lovely lake. We've always wanted a lake, and so we are going to help you find a home.'

'Thank you,' said Giant Jim, and he looked a lot happier. A moment of silence passed and then he asked, 'Have you found one yet?'

'No!' Crasher laughed. 'It will probably take a little bit of time. Come on, Poppy, let's go house-hunting.' Crasher raced off, tripped over his own laces and went crashing all the way to the bottom of the hill.

Poppy ran after him, and the two children spent the rest of the morning searching for a Giant House, and the whole afternoon, and most of the evening too. They had no luck at all. At nine o'clock that night they had to tell Giant Jim that they hadn't found anywhere.

'You will have to stay out here tonight,' said Poppy. 'But I'm sure we will find somewhere for you tomorrow. Will you be all right?'

'Of course I shall,' smiled Giant Jim bravely. 'Giants are always all right. Goodnight.'

3 A Bed for the Night

Night-time came. The sky grew dark and the streets of the town were silent. People switched on their lights and turned on their televisions. Giant Jim sat on the hill and gazed down dreamily at the sleepy town.

Quiet, chirrupy noises came from inside his big wicker basket. 'Oh!' murmured Giant Jim. 'Florence Fluffybum! I forgot all about you. Come on, out you come.' Giant Jim opened the lid of the basket and out stepped Florence Fluffybum.

She had speckled, silvery-grey feathers,
eyes like sparkling glass,
a sticking-up tail,

and long, brown legs with
knibbly-knobbly knees,
and huge splayed toes,
and she was as big as a conker tree.

'Prrrrk,' said Florence Fluffybum,
pecking some food from the ground.
With a flutter of happy-flappy wings,
she jumped on to Giant Jim's head. He
reached up and stroked her soft grey
feathers.

'What are we going to do, Florrie?'
asked Giant Jim.

'Prrrrk,' answered the hen softly.

'Everyone has gone home to bed, and
we are left outside in the dark.'

'Prrrrk,' said Florrie.

'I wish we had a bed and a home.'

'Prrrrk,' said Florrie. The hen glanced
quickly all around. She jumped off Giant

Jim's head and stalked down to the edge
of the town. Florence Fluffybum looked
carefully at every building, which was
quite easy for her, because she was as big
as most of them. Florence Fluffybum
seemed to be looking for something, and
eventually she found it.

40

Florrie lifted her feet carefully, stepped through the town streets and stood outside the library. The library had a great big flat roof. It was just the right place for a giant hen to roost for the night.

'Prrrrrk,' sighed Florrie, climbing on to the roof. She settled her feathers, tucked her head in and closed her eyes.

Giant Jim sadly rubbed his big, ginger beard.

'It's all right for you,' he muttered. 'What about me? Where shall I sleep?'

One by one the night-time stars came out. Giant Jim lay down on the hillside and tried to sleep. He tossed and he turned. He could not make himself comfy at all. He tried counting Farmer Palmer's sheep. He picked them up one by one and put them in another field. 'One, two, three, four . . .'

By the time Giant Jim reached 137
there were no sheep left, so he began
picking up the ducks from the river and
putting them in the cow field. Then he
counted all the cows by picking them up
and putting them in the river, which
came as a bit of a surprise to the cows,
who didn't think it was bath-time at all.
Luckily the river was not deep. The cows
stood there watching the water swirl
slowly round their big fat bellies and
wondered why they felt wet.

Finally Giant Jim gave up trying to sleep. He fetched his saxophone and began playing himself a gentle lullaby. At once windows began opening up and

down the town in every street. Angry
heads poked out and shouted at the
giant. 'Oi! Stop that horrible racket.
We're trying to sleep!' And the
townspeople threw their old boots at
him. They rained down upon the giant
and several boots went right inside his
saxophone, making it go all squeaky.

Giant Jim put down his instrument,
lay on his back and stared up at the
night sky.

'I don't think people like me very much,' he thought. 'They think I'm too big and noisy and clumsy. I can't help it. That's the way I am. If they were all big like me they wouldn't notice.'

He sighed heavily and gazed across the town. His eye caught something interesting and he sat up and looked more carefully.

'I spy a Giant House,' murmured Giant Jim happily, and sure enough there, right on the edge of the little town, stood the Dance Hall, and it was just the right size for a giant.

'All I have to do,' thought Jim, 'is take off the lid.'

He bent down, grasped the roof on both sides and pulled it off, just like taking the lid off a box. Then he lay down inside.

BUT –

– it was dark, and Giant Jim did not see all the chairs and tables, so they all got crushed.

Giant Jim lifted his head and noticed the big stage where the town band always played. 'That will make an excellent resting place for my head,' he sighed happily, and he laid his head upon the stage.

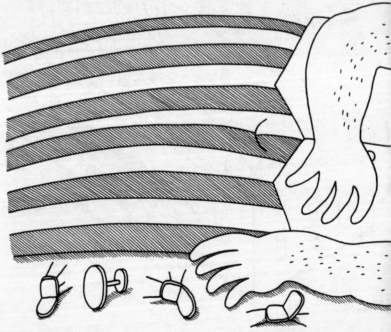

BUT –

– it was dark, and Giant Jim didn't see all the band's instruments lying there, so they all got squashed. There were:

squidged trumpets,
and squodged tubas,
and squoodged flutes,
squeezed oboes, squoozed clarinets,
and squozzlicated trombones.

And as for all the violins – they had been turned into matchsticks.

Giant Jim gave a loud snore, turned on to his side, flattened the drum-set and slept like a child. (A very, very, VERY BIG CHILD!)

4 Disasters Everywhere

Giant Jim slept so well that he did not
wake up until he was disturbed by a
strange roaring noise, and a splashy
feeling all over his face. He opened his
eyes, only to have a bucket of cold water
tossed in his face by Mrs Careless, the
Mayoress.

Behind the Mayoress
stood an angry crowd
of townspeople.

'Look what you've done!' they yelled.
'You've smashed our Dance Hall! You've
smashed all our instruments. We are
supposed to be having our Grand Disco
Dance next week. Now what are we

51

going to do?' And they all began to shout things at Giant Jim.

'You're the biggest, clumsiest oaf in the world!'

'You're the stupidest giant that ever was!'

'And your hen's laid an egg on our library!'

Giant Jim was even more upset than the townspeople. He muttered 'Sorry! I'm sorry!' over and over again. He stood up and tried to mend all the instruments, but he only made matters worse. He tried to put the Dance Hall roof back on, but it crumpled in his hands and all the tiles smashed round his feet, as if he'd just dropped a big bag of marbles.

'Go away!' cried Mrs Careless. 'You giant, ginger, jelly-brain!'

'Leave us in peace!' shouted Mr Sniffling. 'Giants always cause trouble wherever they go, and we don't want trouble here. I want to change my library book,' he complained, 'but I can't because your giant hen is laying eggs on top of the library. Has she got a card? If she hasn't got a library card she's not allowed in the library – or *on* the library,' he added sniffily. Mr Sniffling was backed up by a noisy crowd who shouted that hens weren't allowed in the library anyway.

'You'd better do something,' Poppy Palmer warned Giant Jim.

Giant Jim reached down and picked up Florence Fluffybum, but he was in such a fluster that he dropped her egg and it fell –

KER-SPLATT!

– right on to the library roof, and cracked open. Egg splattered out all over the streets. It dribbled down the library walls and windows.

'Urgh!' yelled Mrs Careless, the Mayoress. 'I've got egg on my best frock.'

'Splurgh!' cried Mr Goodbody. 'I've got egg on my head.'

Farmer Palmer came running up the High Street. 'That stupid giant has put all my sheep in the cornfield, and all my ducks in the cow field, and all my cows in the river!'

'Stupid, stupid giant!' yelled the crowd.

And then someone in the crowd threw an egg at Giant Jim.

It hit the giant on his knee. A jeer went up from the crowd, and a moment later everybody seemed to be throwing eggs at the poor giant and shouting at him and calling him names. He hurried away, clutching Florence Fluffybum, with eggs hitting his back and trickling down to his feet.

Poppy Palmer tried desperately to stop everyone. But nobody could hear her small voice above the cheering and jeering. Poppy stood in the town square, watching the yelling crowd chase after the giant, and tears rolled down her cheeks.

'How can they be so horrid?' she

cried. 'He only wants to be friends.'

Giant Jim stumbled stickily to the edge of the lake. He couldn't bear to feel all that egg and eggshell clinging to him. He plunged into the lake with all his clothes on and started washing frantically. Water began to slop over the edges of the lake.

It sploshed out over the top.
It splished out over the bottom,
and it splashed out all the way
down the edges.

A stream of water began to trickle
towards the town and the more Giant
Jim splashed around, trying to get rid of
all that egg, the more water went down
the hill. Soon the stream became a
brook, and the brook became a river,

and the river became a flood, and the
flood became a –

DISASTER!

'Help!' yelled Mrs Careless, the
Mayoress. 'We're all going to drown!
Now look what you've done!'

'There's a fish swimming round my
living room,' complained Mrs
Goodbody.

'There are frogs hopping up and down
my stairs,' squeaked Mr Sniffling.

Constable Dunstable got out his
bicycle and rode through the wet streets
waving his pair of handcuffs.

'Now I shall really have to arrest the
giant,' he said severely.

Poppy and Crasher were most upset.

'It's not the giant's fault,' they cried.

'He was only trying to get himself clean, and the only reason he was dirty was because you threw eggs at him.'

'Well, he threw an egg at us,' sniffed Mrs Sniffling, 'and it was a very big egg.'

'He didn't throw it. He dropped it and it was an accident. You threw eggs at him on purpose. It's not fair.' Crasher jumped on to his inflatable crocodile and went chasing after Constable Dunstable, crashing into everything on the way.

Nobody would listen to Poppy or Crasher. They were too upset because there was water all over their carpets and their furniture was floating away

down the streets. Some of them pulled on
great rubbery boots and went wading
after the giant. Some of them climbed
into rowing boats and went splashing
after him.

Giant Jim looked out from his giant
bath (which didn't have much water left
in it) and saw the enormous crowd of
townspeople coming after him. They
were waving their fists and shouting

angry words. Some of them were carrying big pieces of wood.

Giant Jim was much, much bigger than any of them, but he was very scared.

'I don't think I like it here any more,' he muttered.

'Don't go!' cried Poppy. 'It's just that they haven't got used to you yet.'

'We all like you!' yelled Crasher, as his crocodile crashed into a tree and got stuck among the branches.

But Giant Jim put Florence Fluffybum back in her basket and strapped his saxophone to his back.

'I thought it would be nice here,' he told Poppy and Crasher. 'I thought I could be helpful and have lots of friends and people to talk to. But I'm too big and clumsy.' He got to his feet and strode away over the far hills and quickly disappeared.

'Hurrah!' shouted the townspeople. 'That got rid of him.'

'It's not fair,' murmured Poppy sadly.

'No, it isn't,' agreed Crasher, and he climbed off his crocodile, fell from the tree and crashed into the flood.

'You silly, clumsy boy!' laughed Mrs Crasher, and she waded into the flood water, rescued her son and gave him a big hug. Crasher turned to her.

'How come when I'm silly you laugh
and give me a hug, but when Giant Jim
is silly you all throw eggs at him and
chase him away?'

Mrs Crasher looked rather surprised.
'I don't really know,' she admitted. 'I
have never thought about it, but I can
tell you one thing. That giant is much
too big to hug.'

5 Help!

Once Giant Jim had gone, things quickly
went back to normal in the town. The
flood waters went down. The houses
dried out. All the animals went back to
the right fields. The library was cleaned.

'What a nice town this is,' said Mrs
Careless, the Mayoress.

'It's clean,' smiled Mr Sniffling.

'It's a peaceful town,' nodded
Constable Dunstable with great
satisfaction.

'That's because it doesn't have a
giant,' said Mrs Goodbody cheerfully.

'It's boring,' muttered little Poppy
Palmer. 'It was much more fun when
Giant Jim was here.'

'Thank goodness he isn't coming

back,' cried Mrs Sniffling. 'We are well rid of him. He was hopeless.' And all the townspeople felt very pleased with themselves because they had got rid of Giant Jim.

But the very next day the hurricane came. It started a long way off. The wind whistled round and round. First of all it spun slowly, picking up dust and specks of dirt and swirling them round. Then it spun faster and grew bigger. It plucked stones and clods of earth from the ground, and whisked them round like beans in a coffee grinder.

The hurricane grew bigger,
and stronger,
and taller,
and wider,
and faster.

Now it was so strong it could pick up dog kennels, and cars, and people on bicycles. It began to twist and turn and snake its way across the countryside, and all the time it was getting stronger and heading straight for the little town.

All at once Farmer Palmer saw half his cows go whizzing up in the air. Round and round they went, like fat brown balloons on legs.

'Help!' yelled Farmer Palmer. 'My cows are flying away! This is even worse than Giant Jim! Everybody hide – the hurricane is here!'

It was truly terrifying. Up in the air
went Farmer Palmer's sheep, a great big
fluffy cloud of them, bleating and
baaing. Then the hurricane hit the town.
Buildings were plucked from the ground
and went swirling round, high in the air.
Some still had people inside.

'Help!' screamed Mr Sniffling, who
was sitting on the toilet when all at once
the whole thing took off like a rocket.
'Put me down! I don't like this. Stop –
I'm getting giddy!'

But the hurricane didn't stop. It
whizzed faster and faster. One by one it

wrenched buildings from the streets of the town and whisked them into the air. Most of the townspeople were running away as fast as they could.

'Save us! Somebody save us!' they screamed as the hurricane came after them, but there was no escape from the great, roaring monster wind.

And then Giant Jim came striding back over the hills from far away. He stopped at the edge of the town and opened his wicker basket. Out jumped Florence Fluffybum. She closed her sparkly eyes against the bitter wind, plonked herself down in front of the hurricane, and dug her strong, sharp claws into the earth so that she could not be blown away.

'You must all hide under Florrie,' shouted Giant Jim. 'You will be safe among her feathers.'

The townspeople pushed and shoved and squeezed and squoozed until they were deeply buried beneath Florence. It was warm and dark and soft.

'It's like being right inside a great big duvet,' whispered Poppy in the darkness.

They couldn't even hear the great hurricane outside, roaring across the countryside, and battering Giant Jim

and Florrie until they felt as if they were locked inside a giant concrete mixer.

The wind whirled round and round Giant Jim. It whistled in his ears. It twisted his hair. It roared right up one giant nostril and then back down the other.

'You can't hurt me!' bellowed Giant Jim. 'I'm a giant and hurricanes are nothing to me!'

It was true too. The hurricane could not hurt him. It went roaring over the hills, away from the little town, and slowly it grew weaker and weaker and weaker, until at last it could not even lift up a ladybird it was so spent.

The townspeople came hurrying out from beneath Florence Fluffybum. 'You saved our lives!' they cried. 'Thank you!' Then they saw their town. At least they

didn't see their town. It had gone. The
hurricane had picked up all the buildings
and whizzed them round and jumbled
them up and set them down anywhere it
felt like.

Some houses were the right way up,
and some houses were on their sides,
and some houses were upside down,
and some houses were piled on top
of each other.

'Oh dear,' sighed Mrs Careless, the Mayoress. 'Now what are we going to do?'

Giant Jim grinned. 'Easy-peasy,' he said. 'I can soon put things right.'

'Be careful,' warned Poppy. 'Don't hold the houses too tightly or you will crush them, just like our Dance Hall.'

With immense care, Giant Jim picked up the houses one by one. Constable Dunstable stood on Giant Jim's shoulder and told him where each house went.

After an hour's hot work the town was almost back to normal. There was only one building left over. It was a great big, empty barn and it stood on top of the hill right next to the little lake. (It was only a little lake now because of Giant Jim's bath.)

'That's not mine,' said Constable Dunstable.

'It's not ours,' said Mr and Mrs Sniffling.

'And it's certainly not one of my barns,' said Farmer Palmer. 'So whose is it?'

'It's a building from nowhere,' murmured Mrs Goodbody.

'It's a Giant House!' shouted Poppy.
'Look – it is just the right size for Giant
Jim.'

And it was too. Giant Jim lay down
inside and the barn roof covered him
over like a great big metal eiderdown.
He grinned back at everyone.

'This is a Giant House,' he chuckled.
'My house!' Then Giant Jim grinned
even more. 'I have an idea. Why don't
you all come to my house, and we shall
have the Grand Disco Dance here, and it
can be a house-warming party too?'

Constable Dunstable frowned. 'It is

kind of you to invite us to your house,
but I think you are forgetting something.
We can't have any music because you
squashed all the band's instruments and
now they can't play anything.'

'Then I shall play my saxophone,' said
Giant Jim, and he did, and everyone fell
over. Then they picked themselves up
and began to dance round and round
and round.

'You are a very kind giant!' cried Mr
Sniffling, waltzing past with Mrs
Sniffling on his arm.

'And you are not stupid at all,' smiled Mrs Careless, the Mayoress, graciously, as she was twirled by Constable Dunstable. 'You're just a bit big, but we are getting used to that now.'

Crasher's Mum sneaked up to Giant Jim, shyly put her arms round one ankle, and gave him a big hug.

Giant Jim played faster and faster, until they were all whirling round like a human hurricane, and Crasher crashed into so many things he felt like a dodgem car.

Even Florence Fluffybum joined in and, as the sun began to set, the giant hen could be seen silhouetted against the skyline, picking up her knobbly brown legs and dancing delicately across the hilltops.

At last, when they were so tired that they could not dance another step, the townspeople made a big bonfire with all the rubbish left over from the hurricane. Giant Jim got out his giant saucepan and cooked scrambled egg for everybody. Then they all got up and started dancing all over again, and that night nobody went home to bed at all, because they were so exhausted that they fell asleep on the hillside – all except for Giant Jim.

He crawled into his Giant House and soon the metal roof was rattling away in time to his giant snores.

Read more in Puffin

For complete information about books available from Puffin – and Penguin – and how to order them, contact us at the appropriate address below. Please note that for copyright reasons the selection of books varies from country to country.

www.puffin.co.uk

In the United Kingdom: Please write to Dept EP, Penguin Books Ltd,
Bath Road, Harmondsworth, West Drayton, Middlesex UB7 ODA

In the United States: Please write to Penguin Putnam Inc., P.O. Box 12289,
Dept B, Newark, New Jersey 07101–5289 or call 1–800–788–6262

In Canada: Please write to Penguin Books Canada Ltd,
10 Alcorn Avenue, Suite 300, Toronto, Ontario M4V 3B2

In Australia: Please write to Penguin Books Australia Ltd,
P.O. Box 257, Ringwood, Victoria 3134

In New Zealand: Please write to Penguin Books (NZ) Ltd,
Private Bag 102902, North Shore Mail Centre, Auckland 10

In India: Please write to Penguin Books India Pvt Ltd,
11 Panscheel Shopping Centre, Panscheel Park, New Delhi 110 017

In the Netherlands: Please write to Penguin Books Netherlands bv,
Postbus 3507, NL–1001 AH Amsterdam

In Germany: Please write to Penguin Books Deutschland GmbH,
Metzlerstrasse 26, 60594 Frankfurt am Main

In Spain: Please write to Penguin Books S. A., Bravo Murillo 19,
1° B, 28015 Madrid

In Italy: Please write to Penguin Italia s.r.l.,
Via Felice Casati 20, I–20124 Milano

In France: Please write to Penguin France S. A.,
17 rue Lejeune, F–31000 Toulouse

In Japan: Please write to Penguin Books Japan, Ishikiribashi Building,
2–5–4, Suido, Bunkyo-ku, Tokyo 112

In South Africa: Please write to Longman Penguin Southern Africa (Pty) Ltd,
Private Bag X08, Bertsham 2013